# Weslandia

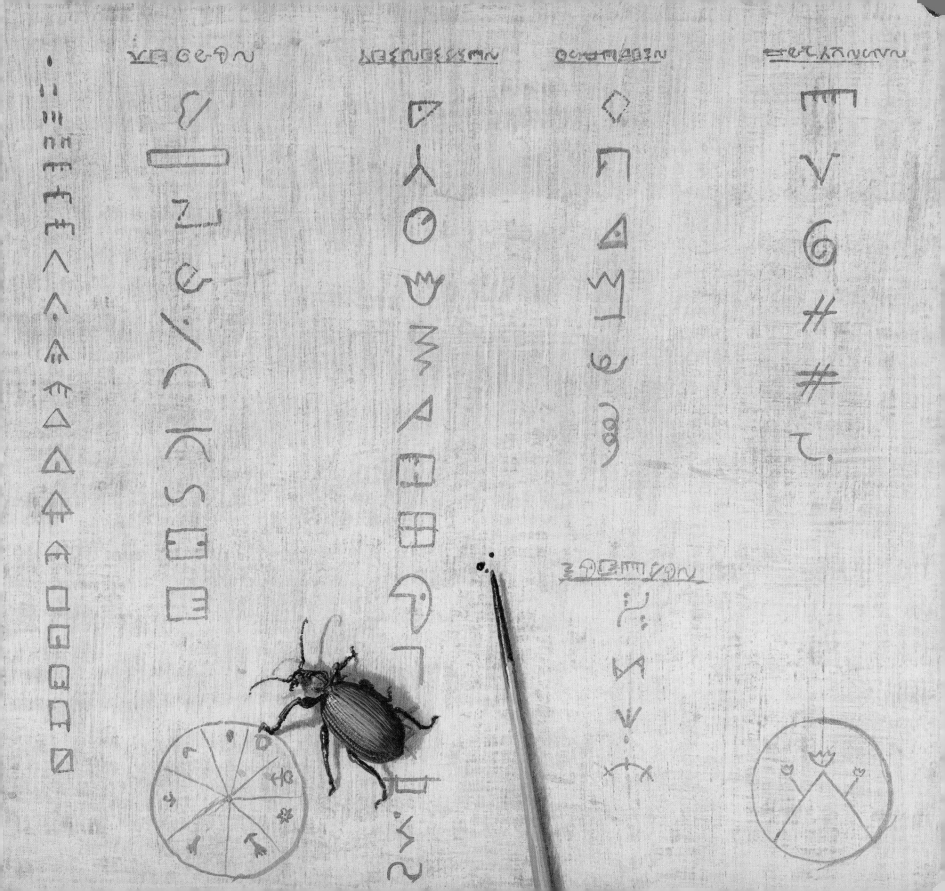

For Clyde Bulla—P. F.

For Greg and Jake,
True Weslandians—K. H.

ISBN 0-439-19270-6

Text copyright © 1999 by Paul Fleischman.
Illustrations copyright © 1999 by Kevin Hawkes. All rights reserved.
Published by Scholastic Inc., 555 Broadway, New York, NY 10012,
by arrangement with Candlewick Press.
SCHOLASTIC and associated logos are trademarks
and/or registered trademarks of Scholastic Inc.

12 11 10 9 8 7 6 5 4 3 2 1          0 1 2 3 4 5/0

Printed in the U.S.A.                    08

First Scholastic printing, September 2000

The book was typeset in Tempus Sans ITC.
The pictures were done in acrylics.

# Weslandia

## PAUL FLEISCHMAN

### ILLUSTRATED BY
### KEVIN HAWKES

SCHOLASTIC INC.
New York  Toronto  London  Auckland  Sydney
Mexico City  New Delhi  Hong Kong

"Of course he's miserable," moaned Wesley's mother. "He sticks out."
"Like a nose," snapped his father.

Listening through the heating vent, Wesley knew they were right. He was an outcast from the civilization around him.

He alone in his town disliked pizza and soda, alarming his mother and the school nurse. He found professional football stupid. He'd refused to shave half his head, the hairstyle worn by all the other boys, despite his father's bribe of five dollars.

Passing his neighborhood's two styles of housing—garage on the left and garage on the right—Wesley alone dreamed of more exciting forms of shelter. He had no friends, but plenty of tormentors.

Fleeing them was the only sport he was good at.

Each afternoon his mother asked
him what he'd learned in school that day.
"That seeds are carried great distances
by the wind," he answered on Wednesday.
"That each civilization has its staple
food crop," he answered on Thursday.
"That school's over and I should find a
good summer project," he answered on Friday.
As always, his father mumbled, "I'm sure
you'll use that knowledge often."

Suddenly, Wesley's thoughts shot sparks. His eyes blazed. His father was right! He could actually *use* what he'd learned that week for a summer project that would top all others. He would grow his own staple food crop— and found his own civilization!

The next morning he turned over a plot of
ground in his yard. That night a wind blew in
from the west. It raced through the trees
and set his curtains snapping. Wesley
lay awake, listening. His land
was being planted.

Five days later the first seedlings appeared.

"You'll have almighty bedlam on your hands if
you don't get those weeds out," warned his neighbor.

"Actually, that's my crop," replied Wesley.
"In this type of garden there are no weeds."

Following ancient tradition, Wesley's fellow gardeners
grew tomatoes, beans, Brussels sprouts, and nothing
else. Wesley found it thrilling to open his land
to chance, to invite the new and unknown.

The plants shot up past his knees,
then his waist. They seemed to be all of
the same sort. Wesley couldn't find
them in any plant book.

"Are those tomatoes, beans, or Brussels sprouts?" asked Wesley's neighbor.
"None of the above," replied Wesley.

Fruit appeared, yellow at first, then blushing to magenta. Wesley picked one and sliced through the rind to the juicy purple center. He took a bite and found the taste an entrancing blend of peach, strawberry, pumpkin pie, and flavors he had no name for.

Ignoring the shelf of cereals in the kitchen, Wesley took to breakfasting on the fruit. He dried half a rind to serve as a cup, built his own squeezing device, and drank the fruit's juice throughout the day.

Pulling up a plant, he found large tubers on the roots. These he boiled, fried, or roasted on the family barbecue, seasoning them with a pinch of the plant's highly aromatic leaves.

It was hot work tending to his crop. To keep off the sun, Wesley wove himself a hat from strips of the plant's woody bark. His success with the hat inspired him to devise a spinning wheel and loom on which he wove a loose-fitting robe from the stalks' soft inner fibers.

Unlike jeans, which he found
scratchy and heavy, the robe was
comfortable, reflected the sun,
and offered myriad opportunities
for pockets.

His schoolmates were scornful, then curious. Grudgingly, Wesley allowed them ten minutes apiece at his mortar, crushing the plant's seeds to collect the oil.

This oil had a tangy scent and served him both as suntan lotion and mosquito repellent. He rubbed it on his face each morning and sold small amounts to his former tormentors at the price of ten dollars per bottle.

"What's happened to your watch?" asked his mother one day.

Wesley admitted that he no longer wore it. He told time by the stalk that he used as a sundial and had divided the day into eight segments— the number of petals on the plant's flowers.

He'd adopted a new counting system as well, based likewise upon the number eight. His domain, home to many such innovations, he named "Weslandia."

Uninterested in traditional sports, Wesley made up his own. These were designed for a single player and used many different parts of the plant. His spectators looked on with envy.

Realizing that more players would offer him more scope, Wesley invented other games that would include his schoolmates, games rich with strategy and complex scoring systems. He tried to be patient with the other players' blunders.

August was unusually hot. Wesley built himself a platform and took to sleeping in the middle of Weslandia. He passed the evenings playing a flute he'd fashioned from a stalk or gazing up at the sky, renaming the constellations.

His parents noted Wesley's improved morale. "It's the first time in years he's looked happy," said his mother.

Wesley gave them a tour of Weslandia.

"What do you call this plant?" asked his father. Not knowing its name, Wesley had begun calling it "swist," from the sound of its leaves rustling in the breeze.

In like manner, he'd named his new fabrics, games, and foods, until he'd created an entire language.

Mixing the plant's oil with soot,
Wesley made a passable ink. As the finale
to his summer project, he used the ink and
his own eighty-letter alphabet to record
the history of his civilization's founding.

In September, Wesley returned to school . . .

He had no shortage of friends.

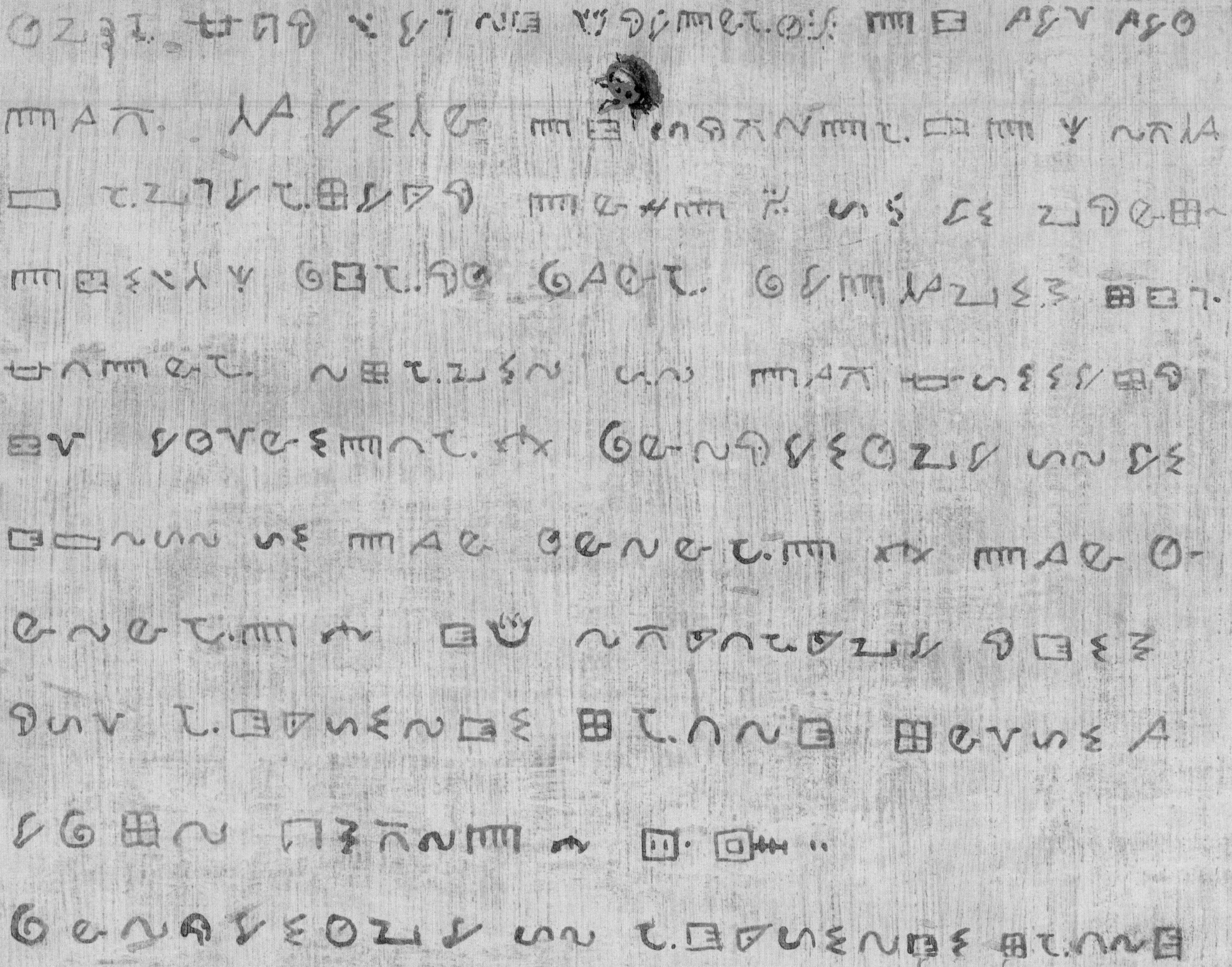

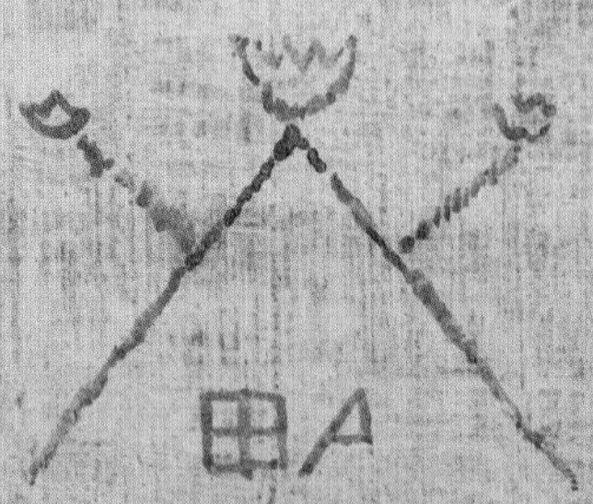

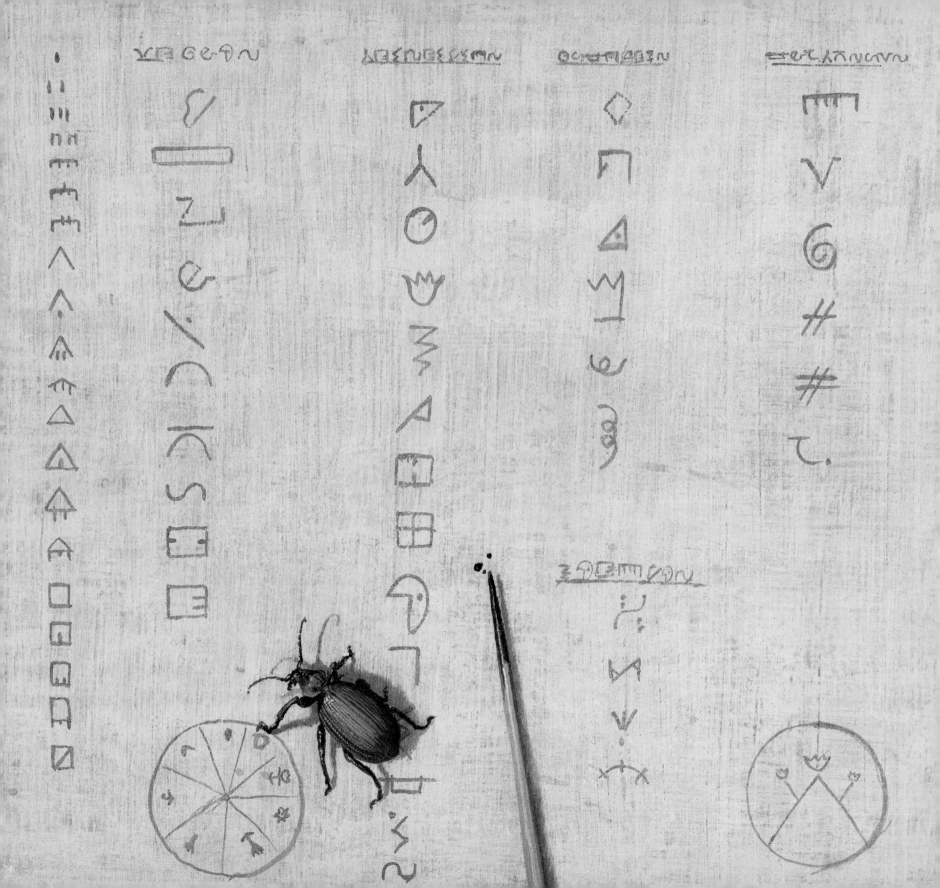